FOR:
Tim, Mike, Annie, Clare,
Lucy, Douglas, Juliet,
James, Anna and Rupert.

POSY SIMMONDS

LULU

and the
FLYING BABIES

PUFFIN BOOKS

I was angry at home....

I was angry in the street....

I was angry in the park...

I shouted in the museum....

We rolled in the snow.....

We splashed in the sea....

We growled at a tiger.....

We patted a King....and gave crisps to his horse.....

We ate some cherries......

...and apples and plums...

...and we spat out the stones down a mountain side....

We got lost in a dark, scary wood.

...**we patted** a **king!** We spat plum stones down a mountain...we got lost in a dark, scary wood....we....

Well I never!